A Note to Parents and Caregivers:

Read-it! Readers are for children who are just starting on the amazing road to reading. These beautiful books support both the acquisition of reading skills and the love of books.

 The PURPLE LEVEL presents basic topics and objects using high frequency words and simple language patterns.

 The RED LEVEL presents familiar topics using common words and repeating sentence patterns.

 The BLUE LEVEL presents new ideas using a larger vocabulary and varied sentence structure.

 The YELLOW LEVEL presents more challenging ideas, a broad vocabulary, and wide variety in sentence structure.

 The GREEN LEVEL presents more complex ideas, an extended vocabulary range, and expanded language structures.

 The ORANGE LEVEL presents a wide range of ideas and concepts using challenging vocabulary and complex language structures.

When sharing a book with your child, read in short stretches, pausing often to talk about the pictures. Have your child turn the pages and point to the pictures and familiar words. And be sure to reread favorite stories or parts of stories.

There is no right or wrong way to share books with children. Find time to read with your child, and pass on the legacy of literacy.

Adria F. Klein, Ph.D.
Professor Emeritus
California State University
San Bernardino, California

To all of my friends who get scared at night ...

First American edition published in 2005 by
Picture Window Books
5115 Excelsior Boulevard
Suite 232
Minneapolis, MN 55416
877-845-8392
www.picturewindowbooks.com

First published in Canada in 2000 by
Les éditions Héritage inc.
300 Arran Street, Saint Lambert
Quebec, Canada J4R 1K5

Printed in the United States of America.

Library of Congress Cataloging-in-Publication Data
St-Aubin, Bruno.
My favorite monster / Bruno St-Aubin.
p. cm. — (Read-it! readers)
Summary: A child discovers that bedtime fears are not as bad as imagined and finds a good
friend in the process.
ISBN 1-4048-1029-3 (hardcover)
[1. Bedtime—Fiction. 2. Monsters—Fiction. 3. Friendship—Fiction. 4. Fear—Fiction.]
I. Title. II. Series.

PZ7.S7743My 2004
[E]—dc22
                                                                    2004023776

My Favorite Monster

Written and Illustrated by
Bruno St-Aubin

Special thanks to our advisers for their expertise:

Adria F. Klein, Ph.D.
Professor Emeritus, California State University
San Bernardino, California

Susan Kesselring, M.A.
Literacy Educator
Rosemount - Apple Valley - Eagan (Minnesota) School District

PiCTURE WiNDOW BOOKS
Minneapolis, Minnesota

Tonight, I don't feel like sleeping.

I'm afraid of the dark.

I don't dare shut my eyes.

It's too dark under my eyelids.

I hear funny noises ...

loud cracking sounds under my bed.

I see shadows on the wall.

I'm so scared my teeth are chattering.

Suddenly, I see something frightening.

A robber!

No, it's not! It's something worse!

A monster is coming at me!

Help! I run as fast as I can.

But I fall into a bottomless pit. I'm done for!

All of a sudden, I stop falling.

The monster has caught me!

What's this?

The monster is wearing my shorts!

The monster is insulted ...

because I'm laughing so hard.

He looks ugly, but he's not mean.

He saved my life!

We decide to be friends.

He invites me into his house.

We visit the places of my dreams.

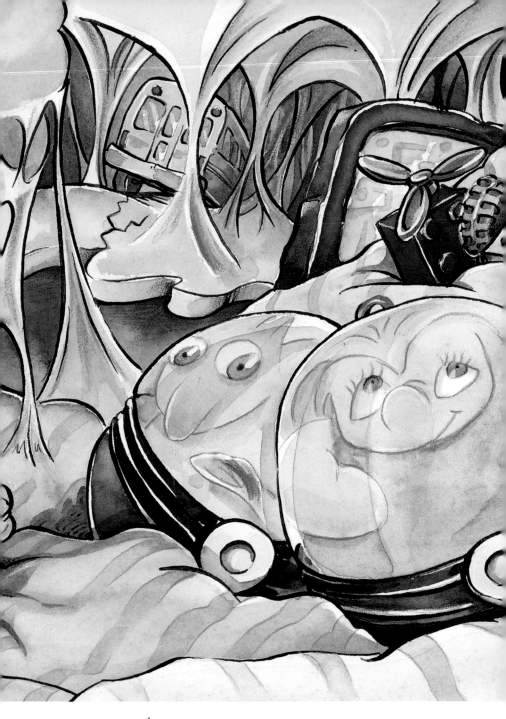

Sometimes they are pretty strange.

I like my monster. He's great!

He's my favorite monster.

More *Read-it!* Readers

Bright pictures and fun stories help you practice your reading skills. Look for more books at your level.

Bamboo at the Beach by Lucie Papineau
The Crying Princess by Anne Cassidy
Eight Enormous Elephants by Penny Dolan
Flynn Flies High by Hilary Robinson
Freddie's Fears by Hilary Robinson
Marvin, the Blue Pig by Karen Wallace
Mary and the Fairy by Penny Dolan
Moo! by Penny Dolan
My Favorite Monster by Bruno St-Aubin
Pippin's Big Jump by Jillian Powell
The Queen's Dragon by Anne Cassidy
Sounds Like Fun by Dana Meachen Rau
Tired of Waiting by Dana Meachen Rau
Whose Birthday Is It? by Sherryl Clark

Looking for a specific title or level? A complete list of *Read-it!* Readers is available on our Web site: *www.picturewindowbooks.com*